GH☁STBUSTERS™

WHO YOU GONNA CALL?

adapted by David Lewman

Ready-to-Read

Simon Spotlight

New York   London   Toronto   Sydney   New Delhi

SIMON SPOTLIGHT

An imprint of Simon & Schuster Children's Publishing Division

1230 Avenue of the Americas, New York, New York 10020

This Simon Spotlight edition June 2016

Ghostbusters TM & © 2016 Columbia Pictures Industries, Inc. All rights reserved.

All rights reserved, including the right of reproduction in whole or in part in any form.

SIMON SPOTLIGHT, READY-TO-READ, and colophon are registered trademarks of Simon & Schuster, Inc.

For information about special discounts for bulk purchases, please contact Simon & Schuster Special Sales at 1-866-506-1949 or business@simonandschuster.com.

Designed by Brittany Naundorff

Manufactured in the United States of America 0516 LAK

10 9 8 7 6 5 4 3 2 1

ISBN 978-1-4814-7501-3 (hc)

ISBN 978-1-4814-7500-6 (pbk)

ISBN 978-1-4814-7502-0 (eBook)

CONTENTS

Chapter 1: Got a Ghost? Get a Ghostbuster!   4

Chapter 2: Meet the Ghostbusters   7

Chapter 3: What Our Crew Can Do for You   18

Chapter 4: Spooky Surprises   28

Chapter 5: Get That Ghost   33

Chapter 6: Busted   38

CHAPTER 1
GOT A GHOST?
GET A GHOSTBUSTER!

Is there someone ghostly in your garage? Or something spooky in your spaghetti? Call us, the Ghostbusters! When it comes to getting rid of ghosts, we're the best!

When you call our headquarters, Kevin will answer right away! He might take longer if he's looking at pictures of himself or playing a game of hide-and-seek.

Eventually, though, Kevin will answer the phone! Then he'll pass your call along to us, the Ghostbusters! (If we're out busting ghosts, Kevin will take a message. Probably. Hopefully.)

When we meet, we'll want to hear everything about your haunting. Even if your story is really weird, we promise not to call you crazy . . . unless, of course, you turn out to be crazy.

CHAPTER 2
MEET THE GHOSTBUSTERS

Now, you may be wondering, who are these Ghostbusters? Where did they come from? Kevin is confused about that too. So let's introduce our all-star team!

ABBY

Abby Yates is the leader of the Ghostbusters. She's studied ghosts her whole life. She loves researching anything paranormal. ("Paranormal" means "not normal" or "weird" or, in our case, "something that makes other scientists laugh at you.") If it's supernatural, Abby's super-excited!

Abby won't rest until she and her team have solved your ghost problem . . . unless a ghost takes over her body—which has happened, but only once. She's totally in control now.

ERIN

Erin Gilbert has been Abby's friend since high school. Erin and Abby even wrote a book together, and they've just written a second one! You could say that Erin "wrote the book on ghosts" (because she did . . . with Abby . . . twice).

Erin's a brilliant scientist. She's also brave. She was the first Ghostbuster to blast a ghost! And she's ready to blast your ghost too! *ZAP!*

HOLTZMANN

Jillian Holtzmann is the Ghostbusters' brilliant engineer. That means she's in charge of building all our tools, proton packs, PKE meters, ghost traps—you name it! She's also in charge of fixing our gizmos when they break. She enjoys anything that burns or explodes.

Holtzmann is smart, courageous, and fiercely loyal. She also loves a good fart joke. Especially if it's a ghost fart!

PATTY

Patty Tolan used to work for the New York subway system. (In fact, she sometimes wishes she still did. Ghostbusting doesn't pay very well.) But it got lonely sitting in a ticket booth all day, so she joined the Ghostbusters.

Patty is our expert on the history of New York City. She has read almost every book on the subject. She can tell you where ghosts gather and why. We also have Patty to thank for our awesome ride! (Wait until you see our car!)

15

KEVIN

Kevin is the Ghostbusters' receptionist. When he first came to work for us, he didn't know much about ghosts. To tell the truth, he still doesn't, but he's eager to help! He has a motorcycle, the Ecto-2, in case we need backup. (We never need backup.)

CHAPTER 3
WHAT OUR CREW CAN DO FOR YOU

You might be saying, "Sure, this is a team of highly trained professionals, but what do they bring to the party?"

The answer is: tons! When you hire the Ghostbusters, we'll bring the very latest in ghostbusting equipment. (Not the safest, but the latest.) We'll come to you loaded down with detectors, recorders, cameras, proton packs, proton wands—the works!

All our stuff is kept in tip-top
shape by Holtzmann, because when
there's a screaming ghost flying
at you, there's really no time for
equipment problems!

How do we reach our clients, you ask? We zoom to any haunted location in our special ghost-hunting car loaded with ghostbusting features! Just look for the Ecto-1 license plate.

NEW YORK

ECTO-1

"Ecto" stands for "ectoplasm," which is the sticky ooze left behind by ghosts. It's pretty slimy. Why do you think we wear easy-to-clean jumpsuits?

You may notice that our car used to be a hearse, the kind of car you'd see at a funeral. Some people think that's creepy. For our line of work, we think it makes sense!

Once we find a parking space big enough for the Ecto-1, we run, or walk, right into the haunted location, carrying our equipment . . .

. . . which is very heavy. Feel free
to help us. Holtzmann's working on
making the gear lighter, but for now
it weighs one thousand pounds.
Seriously.

For those ghosts that like to play hide-and-seek, we send in Kevin! (Just kidding! We would never send in Kevin.) With our PKE meters and hard-earned experience, we can find any ghost before you can say "Boo!"

Teachable moment! Did you know that ghosts don't say "boo"? That's just a myth. Ghosts usually glare at people in silence or scream really, really loudly. You already knew that? Well, of course you did! You're being haunted.

Once we find the ghost, it's smooth sailing—for the ectoplasm, that is. The ooey, gooey gunk usually flies out of the otherworldly entity and lands all over us!

It can be a little scary when ghosts appear, and when they scream and slime. But do the Ghostbusters turn around and run out of the building screaming for help?

Not unless it's absolutely necessary.
We hate leaving behind our gear.

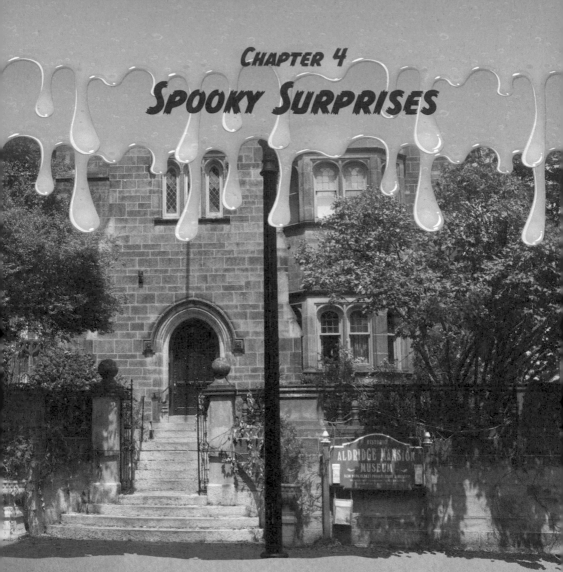

CHAPTER 4
SPOOKY SURPRISES

Now, folks, one thing's for sure
about the ghostbusting business:
it's full of surprises! Ghostbusters
have to be ready for anything. You
never know where (or when) ghosts
are going to pop up.

In fact, sometimes ghosts think it's funny to sneak up on us slowly or float silently! If this happens while we're investigating your haunting, please inform us immediately. Or just scream. We'll get the message.

We are pros at dealing with ghosts in unlikely places—like inside our employees! A ghost once took over Kevin's body. This is called "possession." The ghost made Kevin dance like a disco star. This is called "embarrassing."

Don't worry, we got rid of the ghost in no time. Now Kevin's completely back to normal — we think.

So, you see, there is no team better fit to deal with spooky surprises than the Ghostbusters. We even have a few tricks up our sleeves! For example, ghosts can't haunt you if they can't find you! Isn't that hilarious?

See if you can spot Holtzmann in this picture from our Stonebrook Theater case.

CHAPTER 5
GET THAT GHOST

In all seriousness, clients don't come to the Ghostbusters for fun and games. (Hide-and-seek, anyone?) They come to us for results! So once we've made contact with a "visitor from the other side" (that means a ghost), we get down to business. Ghostbusting business!

We catch ghosts using our proton packs, wands, and traps. We line up and reach for our wands.

Next it's ready . . . aim . . . BLAST!
We hit them with a crackling stream
of positive proton energy! Ghosts
hate that.

Now for the fun part. It's pretty
amazing to see us trap a ghost,
but we don't recommend hanging
around when we're firing our wands.

Because . . . (Please turn the page.)

It can get a little messy!

When we blast a ghost with a high-energy stream of protons, lots of things can happen. Almost all of them involve ectoplasm spraying everywhere! Yuck!

Teachable moment! Never open your mouth wide when slime is splattering all over you. It tastes terrible. Trust us.

CHAPTER 6

BUSTED

Are you ready to see how we really earn our money? Using our proton wands, we pull the ghost down into the special trap!

Then we check the readings on
the trap to make sure the ghost is
inside, and we celebrate!
WHOO-HOO! WE JUST BUSTED
ANOTHER GHOST! TIME TO PARTY!

So if you're being haunted by a phantom, apparition, boogeyman, spirit, specter, or plain old ghost, don't panic. Just reach for the phone.

WHO YOU GONNA CALL?